A
Secret
Between Friends

L.L. River

PublishAmerica
Baltimore

ISBN: 1-60563-720-3
PUBLISHED BY PUBLISHAMERICA, LLLP
www.publishamerica.com
Baltimore

Printed in the United States of America

Prologue

"Oh, Gabe, please."

"Please what?" Gabriel whispered into his dream lover's ear.

"Please, Gabe, please, don't stop making love to me."

"Say my name again," he growled into her ear as he slid deeper into her.

"No," she managed to squirm out.

"Say it, please."

"Gabriel, Gabriel," the woman purred in Gabriel's ear.

"I've waited for ten years to have you whisper in my ear," Gabriel said. He crushed his mouth on hers and they climaxed together. Gabriel wanted this night to last forever. He had finally gotten the woman of his dreams into his bed. Now he had to a find a way to keep her there forever. She'd been in his dreams almost every night since he was twelve years old. He thought he was dreaming now until he felt her move underneath him. He kissed her forehead and rolled off of her.

"I have to go," she said as she got out of bed.

"You just got here two hours ago," he said trying to pull her back into the bed.

"Look, Gabe, you were great, but I have to go. I came here with someone else," she said as she looked around the room for her clothes.

"I thought you said you came here with friends," Gabe said when he jumped out of the bed and grabbed her by the wrist.

"I did, but...uh," She stammered out.

"But what?" Gabriel asked threw gritted teeth.

"One of the friends is a man that I'm considering dating," she said as she looked away from his stare.

"I've wanted you almost all my life," Gabriel said in a low voice when he let her wrist go and turned away from her.

"What?" She stammered as she dropped her dress that she had picked up to put back on.

"I've wanted you for myself since I was twelve years old. I can't believe I slept with you. I've dreamed about you for years and now you're in my bed. I'm in love with you and I always have been."

"Gabe, you know we can't be together. You have to promise me you want ever tell anyone that we slept together. You were the most incredible lover I've ever had and I'm glad that we ran into one another," she said as she put her dress on.

"So, I was a good fuck and now you're done with me and you're going to go back to the guy you came with," he growled.

"Don't talk to me like that. You knew I had to leave right afterwards, because I told you before we slept together.

I'm not trying to hurt you, but I have to go and you can't tell anyone especially you're sister."

"So this is it? I see you're still the same girl you've always been," he said angrily.

"What is that suppose to mean?" She said as she walked back to the bed to put on her shoes.

"When you were in high school I always heard guys talk about how easy you were and it made me so mad. I was only twelve, but I knew what they meant. Now I know what they were saying was true," he said and grabbed her by the arm, "How many men have you slept with since you arrived in town?"

"Gabe, you're hurting my arm," she whimpered.

"I'm sorry," he said releasing her arm.

"Gabe, you have to believe me when I say that you were the best lover I've ever had, but now I have to go. My friends are waiting for me."

"Don't leave me damn it, I need you," Gabe said in a very emotional voice.

"Gabe, please, don't do this to me. I didn't mean for this to happen, but it did and it was great. Promise me you want tell you're sister she'll never forgive me if she found out. I'm so proud of you for graduating at the top of your class. I always knew you were smart and you're going to be very successful," the woman said as a single tear rolled down her face.

"Was fucking me my graduation present?" Gabriel asked as he started to pace around the room.

"That's not true, please don't think that," the woman pleaded.

"Does your man know that you're up her right now with me? He must be use to sharing you with other men by now."

"That isn't fair," the woman said as she struggled to hold back more tears from falling down her face.

"Almost all my life I've admired and loved you. I was so happy when you would come over to visit my sister because I knew you would wear those little shorts and I loved your beautiful long legs. You were so damn sexy. I wanted to eat you alive. I've had dirty dreams about you since as far as I can remember back. I would ask my sister everyday If you were going to come over to visit. You made my day. You were absolutely beautiful. You've had me since the moment I laid eyes on you."

"Gabe, please don't say anymore."

"I was jealous whenever I saw you with a guy, because in my head you were my woman. I was only twelve so I knew I didn't have a chance in hell with you. I'm a grown man now and I still can't have you. I was a 22 year old virgin until two hours ago," he whispered.

"You mean I took you're virginity," she cried. Damn, can a woman take a man's virginity?

"Yes you did and I feel awful because now I know that everything I use to hear about you was true. We didn't even use protection and there's no telling what I may have contracted from you. You were a slut then and you're a slut now," he yelled at her while pulling on his clothes.

"Gabe, you don't mean that," she said near sobs.

"Yes, I do and you don't have to worry about me telling my sister about this, because as far as I'm concerned it never happened and you no longer exist. You want hear from me again unless the many test that I'll be taking come back positive," Gabe said and left the woman that took his virginity sobbing in the hotel room.

Chapter One

Two years later.

Crystal Sterner waited at the airport for her best friend to arrive. She was so excited because they hadn't seen each other in four years. They kept contact with each other, but their schedules wouldn't allow them time to see one another. They hadn't seen one another since they graduated with their bachelor's degree. Crystal couldn't wait for her best friend to arrive. She had so much to talk to her about. When should I tell her about my brother's awful mood? She's bound to notice something is wrong with him. Her thoughts were interrupted she heard someone yell her name. She turned around and she was looking at her beautiful best friend Heather Kenley. Heather looked just like a supermodel probably because she was. Heather was five feet ten inches and she weighed one hundred twenty-pounds. Her wavy jet-black hair came to the middle of her back and it was now highlighted with gold streaks. Her face was perfectly shaped; as were her eyebrows and her eyes were the color of green emeralds and they were sparkling as they had since she was a child. Her skin was flawless as ever and she looked every part of the Supermodel she was. She was wearing a fitted thigh length Calvin Klein dress and her legs looked about a mile long. Crystal had never seen her look more gorgeous. She knew as soon as her little brother took one look at her best friend, his tongue was going to hang out of this head. It was going to be a joy to watch. Could her best friend ever love her little brother? This I can't wait to see. Crystal thought to herself. They embraced each other and started crying.

"I've missed you so much," Heather said to her.

"I've missed you too," Crystal said, "I have so much to tell you and we have so much to catch up on. I'm so glad that you're here," Crystal said in heavy tears.

"Crystal, what's the matter?" Heather asked with concern.

"Nothing I'm just really glad that you're here that's all. My parents can't wait to see you and guess who else is at our house to see you?" Crystal said.

"Who?" Heather said in a panicked voice.

"You're high school sweetheart Ricky Banes. He was so excited when he found out that you we're coming to visit. I think he still loves you Heather. Are you seeing anybody?" Crystal asked.

"I'll tell you everything later. Let's just go to your house so I can see your parents," Heather said as they were walking to his car.

"Heather, aren't you forgetting someone else that's you didn't mention?"

"Yes, your brother. How is he?" Heather asked not looking into her best friends eyes.

"Well, he's in a really bad mood, so you may want to stay away from him," Crystal said in a sad voice.

"What's the matter with him?"

"We have no clue; because he won't tell us anything. I don't feel like taking about him now. I want to enjoy our time together. By the way, he hates Ricky and he's dating your high school rival," Crystal said avoiding Heather's stare.

"You mean you're little brother is dating Skyler Green, the town slut, and you're parents are allowing it?" Heather said in disbelieve.

"He's a grown man what can they do?"

"I guess they can't do anything and why does he hate Ricky?"

"I have no clue, but he may not be there when you arrive and if he has that really mean look on his face you may want to stay away from him," Crystal said as they got into the car.

"Okay, I'll try to stay away from him. I can't wait to see your parents. I've really missed everybody and I really want to take a nap," Heather said rolling down her window. A frown came to her face when she thought of Sklyer Green. When Heather was in high school, Skyler Green was her worst enemy. Skyler was a pretty girl; she had fiery red hair that came to her shoulders. She had dark green eyes and even though she was a red-head she didn't have a face full of freckles. In high school Skyler constantly tried to humiliate Heather because of where she came from. Everyone knew that Heather wasn't from the riches family and her Father had to work double over-time to get her the clothes she wanted and Mother was jealous of her because of her beauty and her Mother occasionally drank too much and Skyler made sure no one ever forgot that. But regardless of all the things Skyler tried to do to hurt Heather, she never succeeded. Heather was still the most popular girl in school and she dated the best-looking guy, Ricky Banes. Ricky was the guy all the girls wanted and he wanted Heather and they had dated almost the entire time they were in high school together. Ricky was tall and handsome and sweet and the star of the football and baseball team. He had dark brown hair and hazel eyes and he was all muscle even though he was in high school. He was an all American white boy and he was all Heather's when they were in high school. He was also the guy that Skyler Green wanted most but couldn't have. She had tried everything in her power to break Heather and Ricky up and it never worked, accept once and Ricky dumped Heather immediately. He dated Skyler after the break-up just to get to Heather. The break-up lasted for about five months or so and they were both miserable and Heather slept with Ricky's friend when she heard that he had slept with Skyler. Then she found out it was a big lie and she had slept with Ricky's friend for nothing and she had felt like a whore and she refused to talk to him for months afterwards because of how dirty she felt. Ricky forgave and they had gotten back together, but they parted ways when they graduated.

"Well, as soon as you see everybody you can nap sleeping beauty. I saw you on the cover of Belle Magazine and you were absolutely gorgeous. I think my dad drooled over the cover for hours and mom laughed so hard when she caught him staring at it. They are so proud of you and don't tell my brother I told you, but I saw him sleep with the magazine for several days. He's still smitten by you after all these years," Crystal said smiling at her Heather and bringing her away from her thoughts.

"What do you mean?" Heather asked in a daze.

"You know my brother has always had a crush on you. I hope your being here will cheer him up," Crystal said squeezing her best friends arm.

"Thank you so much dear for saying that dear," But that's hardly likely Heather thought to herself. She leaned back into seat and looked at her best friend and smiled to herself. Oh, how opposite they were, but so similar at the same time. Crystal was about five feet five, with strawberry blond hair, and blue eyes. She never wore revealing clothes, and she was to Heather knowledge still a virgin. Heather was the wild one and she was the quiet calm one, but she did get a little wild on a couple of occasions Heather swore to her that she would never tell anyone about. She laughed to herself and looked out the window and thought about how things would be when she saw Gabriel again for the first time in two years.

They arrived ten minutes later at the Sterner Estates. Heather was short of breathe when she saw Crystal's younger brother standing outside with his mother and father. Gabriel Sterner was without a doubt one of the best looking men Heather had ever seen in her life. When he was younger she just looked at him as being her best friends annoying little brother that hung around her as often as he could. She knew he liked to look at her long legs and rub on them and pretend it was accidental. But they way she looked at him changed when he turned eighteen and he became a man. He had turned into a beautiful man. He was six feet two inches, all muscle. He had piercing blue eyes like his sister and their father. His hair was light brown with streaks of blond. He had a scar above his right eye from when he trying to be a dare devil in his early days to impress her and landed himself in the hospital for five days with a stitched up head and a concussion. She had cried herself to sleep the night that happened. She felt it was all her fault that he was hurt. Earlier that day she had told him that he was only a little boy and that he should stop trying to hang around her and Crystal and that it was very annoying to have a little twerp around when they were trying to have girl talk. Two hours later they were rushing to the hospital. She had never forgiven herself for that and she had caused him pain once again. She could tell by the look on his face handsome face he was still in pain and he hated her. Crystal parked the car and they both got out. Heather was embraced by both of Crystal's parents, but

Gabriel just gazed at her. When they let her go she was embraced by Ricky and he held her for a very long time.

"I've missed you so much," he whispered to her.

"I've missed you all so much. Thank you for being here to welcome me back home," Heather said as she inched away from Ricky, she didn't like the way Gabriel was looking at them.

"Heather, you look so beautiful and very tired. Would you like to rest now dear?" Mrs. Sterner said sweetly.

"Yes, I would, where is my room?" Heather asked Mr. Sterner.

"You'll be staying in the room next to Gabe's. Gabe, help Heather with her bags please son."

"No problem dad anything for the beautiful wonderful Heather," Gabriel said sarcastically.

"I'll take your bags Heather," Ricky said running over to pick up her bags.

"Why thank you so much Ricky. You were always such a gentleman," Heather said kissing him on the cheek. Gabe muttered something under his breath and everyone pretended not to hear it. What is this asshole doing here to greet my woman anyway? Gabriel thought to himself. I should kick his ass. What did she ever see in him? So what if he looks like a damn GQ model, I know I was better in bed. She was screaming my name and clawing her nails in my back and I made her climax like five times and look at this bastard. He's looking at her like he wants to eat her alive and I'm damn sure I'm looking at her the same way. I wonder if she's slept with him since high school. I bet she has, why else would he be here looking at her like that? I'll kill them both if she goes out with him and doesn't come back until late at night. Damn, she's only gotten prettier over the past two years. She's glowing like she always has and I'm more in love with her than ever.

"Well, Gabe still needs to show you to the room. We've changed around so much since you're last visit dear," Mrs. Sterner said to Heather.

"I'd love a tour after my nap," Heather said as she kissed Mr. and Mrs. Sterner on the cheek.

"We're so proud of you Heather and we're so happy that you're here to visit us," Mr. Sterner said.

"You've always been like a daughter to us and we love you very much. Now you go in the house and get some rest," Mrs. Sterner said to Heather.

"Crystal, I have so much to tell you later. I'll see you when I wake up. I was hoping to take you and Gabe to dinner tonight if you don't mind?" Heather said to Crystal and Gabe.

"Heather, I was going to have a special dinner prepared for you tonight," Mrs. Sterner said.

"Well, that sounds wonderful and it saves me money," Heather said and everyone started to laugh except for Gabe.

"Am I invited Mrs. Sterner?" Ricky asked.

"Of course you are dear," Mrs. Sterner said sweetly.

"I can't make the dinner tonight," Gabe said in a menacing voice

"Why not son?" Mr. Sterner asked his son in a voice very close to anger.

"I have a date tonight and I'm going to get laid dad. Aren't you happy that I'm not sulking around anymore?" Gabe said very disrespectfully.

"Gabriel Sterner, how dare you talk like that in front of your mother? I raised you better than that young man and if you continue to act this way you'll find yourself out on your ass. I don't know what's the matter with you, but you'd better show some respect. Heather just arrived and I think her being here is more important than some date," Mr. Sterner said angrily.

"I'll show Heather to her room dad," Crystal said trying to break the tension.

"I'll do it," Gabriel said interrupting Crystal.

"Alright, I'll see everyone at dinner," Crystal said and kissed everyone on the cheek.

"Mom, I'm sorry for what I said. Do you forgive me?" Gabe said before he went into the house.

"Of course I do son. I'll see you at dinner right?"

"Yes mother," Gabe said and went into the house. Heather and Ricky followed behind. The room Heather was staying in at the end of the hall next to Gabe's.

"This is your room. I hope you enjoy the bed with Ricky," He said nastily and left them alone.

"What crawled up his ass?" Ricky said as he put Heather's bags down.

"I have no idea. How have you been Mr. Banes?" Heather asked sitting on the bed and taking off her shoes.

"I'm doing great. My career is going great. I'm in the technology field and I really love it. I saw you on the cover of that magazine last month and you were absolutely stunning."

"Thank you so much Ricky. It was a very nice photo shoot and I was very happy about the outcome. I couldn't believe I was on the cover of a magazine. I've all ready been asked to do four more magazine covers. As soon as my vacation is over I have about seven photo-shoots to do."

"Wow that's amazing. You are prettier than I remembering you being. I never thought you could any prettier, but I was wrong. You're absolutely stunning. I'm going to go now and let you get your beauty sleep. I'll see you at dinner."

"Thank you again for being here to welcome me back," Heather said getting up from the bed and hugging him tightly.

"You can always count on me Heather. You'll always have a special place in my heart. I'll see you later," he said and left the room. Heather smiled to herself and walked over the vanity and sat down and started to brush her hair. She closed her eyes for a minute and she thought of her night when she made love with Gabriel Sterner.

Chapter Two

Two years earlier.

"Heather, hi, what are you doing here?" Someone called out to her from behind. She turned around and her heart stopped. It was Gabriel Sterner. Her best friend's younger brother and he was not little anymore. He was all male and he was handsome as ever. He looked as if he had just come from a late night party and he had been drinking. As he walked closer to her she smelled his cologne. It was a wonderful scent and it was touched with cigar smoke and a mixed drink. It was a wonderful combination.

"Gabe, hi," she said breathlessly. He stopped within inches from her face and put his arms around her waist and hugged her tight. She thought he would kiss her on the cheek but he kissed her on the lips and he kissed her longer than he should have.

"Oh, well, nice to see you too," Heather said blushing to the roots of her hair.

"You look delicious Heather, what are you doing here?" He asked as he kept his arm around her waist and looked at her like he wanted to eat her alive. Her insides started to melt.

"Just taking a mini vacation with some friends and you?" She asked in a low husky voice.

"I just graduated from college and I'm here celebrating with friends as well," he said as he pointed to his friends across the room. They saw them watching them from across the room started walking over.

"Gabe, how do you know this celebrity?" His friend Carl asked him as he stared at Heather in awe.

"This is my sisters best friend, I've know her since I was a kid."

"You lucky bastard," his other friends Darrel said.

"Yes I am, Heather these are my friends Carl, Thomas, Arron, Mike, and Darrel," Gabe said as he introduced Heather to his friends.

"Hi." They all said in unison.

"Hi, nice to meet you all. Are you guys having a good time in Vegas?" Heather asked them.

"We are now, you are damn gorgeous. I saw you in last months aid for CK, was that your first time modeling?" Thomas asked her as he stared at her like he wanted to take a bite out of her.

"Yes, was it that obvious?" Heather asked as she giggled at Thomas.

"No, it just that, that was my first time seeing you in an aid that's all."

"Okay guys, go do whatever it is you were doing and stop drooling over my Heather," Gabe said as he pulled Heather away from his friends that were ogling over her.

"Nice meeting you guys," Heather called to them as she was being led away.

"Same here." They all said as they watched her walk away in complete awe.

"This is my first time in Vegas. And you know what they say, what happens in Vegas, stays in Vegas," Gabe said when he pulled Heather into a corner and took her into his arms and winked at her, "What are you about to do?"

"Um...I....uh...I don't know," what's the matter with me? I'm acting like a damn school girl. I'm a grown woman damn it and this is just Gabe. Crystal's little brother.

"Come to my room with me," he said as he kept his hold on her.

"What?" Heather stammered out nearly fainting.

"You heard me, I said come to my room with me," he whispered into her ear.

"Gabe, I don't think that's a good idea. You're here with friends and I'm here with someone else. It wouldn't be a very good idea."

"Why not, I just want to talk to you and catch up on things and have a few drink, there's no harm in that, is there?" He asked as he started to walk her towards the elevator.

"I guess not, if that's all you have in mind."

"Why Heather, what else would I have in mind?" He asked with a wicked grin on his handsome face.

"I don't know, you tell me," she said when she moved away from him and leaned into the wall of the elevator.

"You know what I want from Heather, you've known for years, but I want do anything to you, you don't want me too," he said when he moved to wrap his hand around the back of her neck in lightning speed.

"Gabe, this shouldn't happen."

"Nothing's happened, yet," he tipped her head back and kissed her lightly on the lips. She moaned out.

"Gabe, please," she said barely above a whisper.

"Mine room or yours?"

"Mine on the eighteenth floor," she said breathlessly. He reached his hand over and pushed in the eighteenth floor and then he kissed her more passionately than she had ever been kissed in her life. He took her breath away.

"I'm going to make love to you Heather and I'm going to do you better than you've ever been done before," Gabriel whispered into her ear when he removed his mouth from hers.

"This can only happen tonight and never again do you understand that?"

"Yes, I know and that's all I need," the elevator stopped and he carried her off and into her room. Once they made it inside, he put the do not disturb sign on the door, and shut the door, and it did not open for hours.

Present day.

"You're done with him all ready. That was pretty fast, he must be one of those fast ones," Gabe said interrupting Heathers daydream.

"What?" Heather stammered out when she opened her eyes.

"You heard me," Gabriel said.

"What do you want Gabe? I'm really tired and I don't want to hear your bullshit right now. Get out of here," Heather said with a yawn.

"Did you fuck him in my parent's home?" Gabe growled at her.

"Gabe, please leave me alone. I'm very tired and I don't have time for this," Heather said turning her back on him.

"You haunted my dreams for two years and you've turned me into a basket case. I'm moody all the time and I haven't sleep with another woman in two years. My family hates to be around me, because I'm so mean and rude. You've ruined my life are you happy? Are you? Answer me damn it," Gabe said and then he realized Heather was sound asleep. He peeled off her clothes and put the covers over her. He watched her sleep for several hours, "Damn you Heather for ruining my life," he said when he finally left the room.

Chapter Three

"Crystal, how long have I been asleep?" Heather asked when she looked up and saw it was dark outside. Then she looked down and noticed her clothes were off. How did my clothes get off?

"You've been asleep for four hours. I came to make sure you were still breathing. I didn't mean to wake you up sleeping beauty. Nice rack," Crystal said looking at Heather's exposed breast.

"Thanks, can you pass me my T-shirt? I didn't mean to sleep this long. I guess I didn't realize how tired I was. When is dinner going to be ready?"

"Not for another two hours. We can catch up on things while dinner is being prepared. What do you say to that?" Crystal asked eagerly as she passed Heather her T-shirt.

"Sounds great to me; you go first my dear," Heather said sitting up in the bed putting on her T-shirt.

"Before I tell you the goods on myself; I came in earlier to check on you and my brother was watching you sleep. I knew your being here would make him feel better. You should've seen how he was looking at you. It was very beautiful. It was almost as if he's in love with you, but that's ridiculous right?"

"Of course it is," Heather said feeling uncomfortable.

"I can't believe that your here. My best friend is a damn supermodel. I think that's awesome. How is Ricky doing? What did you guys talk about?" Crystal said getting comfortable in the bed next to Heather.

"Nothing really, just about my modeling and his career; he looks so damn good. Too bad I kind of have a fiancé or I may have hooked up with him before I left," Heather said with a devilish grin on her face.

"You're so bad Heather. Oh my goodness, you said you have a fiancé. I can't believe that. How long have you been engaged? Why didn't you tell me as soon as you arrived, you bitch?" Crystal said hugging Heather.

"I said I'm sort of engaged. This is just a promise ring. We're not officially engaged yet. I haven't given him an answer yet. His name is Stephen Daniels and we've been dating for two years and he's incredible."

"Oh, he must be really good in bed. Do you love him Heather?" Crystal cried happily.

"I don't know Crystal, I just don't know. I guess that's why I haven't answered him yet. He's such a good man and he treats me like a princess. I don't know why I'm not in love with him. You want to know a secret."

"What is it?" Crystal asked with all ears.

"We've never slept together. Can you believe that?" Heather asked her best friend.

"No, I can't. You've been dating him two years and you haven't done it. I know you and you'd never go for that," Crystal said honestly.

"I haven't had sex in two years and I haven't wanted to. I have to ask you something and I want you to tell me the truth okay?" Heather said on the verge of tears.

"Okay, what is it?"

"Did you think I was a slut when we were in high school?"

"Heather, why would you ask me something like that?" Crystal asked jumping out of the bed.

"Answer the question Crystal. Did you think that?"

"Of course I didn't think that. Who told you that?" Crystal asked angrily.

"Did everyone else think that?"

"No, and whoever told you that is a fucking liar. I know you slept with a couple of guys in high school and they may have talked about it, but no one thought you were a slut. Everyone loved you and you know that. How else could you have won Homecoming and Prom Queen?" Heather asked with a grin on her face.

"Oh, be quiet you. That was by luck that I won both. I had forgotten all about winning those. I only slept with two guys when I was in high school and that was Ricky and John. I did have a lot of sex, but that was only with the two of them. I slept with Ricky almost every day that we dated. We only took a break when I was on my period. He was horny as a rabbit and he would hump my brains out every chance he got," Heather said laughing.

"You must know that I never thought you were a slut. You're my best friend and I love you dearly. How in the

27

world have you gone two years without sex?" Crystal asked.

"I have no idea, but after seeing Ricky I'm really horny. I may sneak out tonight and find him." Heather said and they laughed together, "So who are you dating? You're still not a virgin are you?"

"Heather, I'm 27 years old; of course I'm not a virgin anymore. I had sex for the first time two weeks ago and you'll never guess who it was."

"Spill it," Heather said excitedly.

"It was Kenneth Elliott and we did it in at the park downtown after hours and he was awesome. He did me real good and then we had sex again two days later," Crystal said blushing.

"Wow! You slept with Kenneth Elliott. I never thought he would be your type. I bet he was awesome in bed. So, are you guys dating or just fucking?" Heather asked in a teasing voice.

"We've been dating for six months and I just had to have him. I couldn't go anymore without him being inside of me," Crystal said blushing again.

"You're in love with him aren't you?" Heather asked happily

"Yes, I am and it feels very wonderful. I've never been in love before and I like how it feels," Crystal said with a tear in her eyes.

"I can't believe you're seeing Kenneth Elliott. He was such a bad ass in school. I mean he was terrible. He always got into trouble and he was arrested like a dozen times. I never thought you would go for him," Heather said smiling at Crystal.

"Do you think dating him is a bad idea?" Crystal asked.

"Is he like he was when he was in high school?" Heather asked squeezing her best friend's hand.

"He's changed a lot, but he's still a bad ass. My bad ass and I love him. You want to know a secret that I've never told you?" Crystal asked with a happy smile on her face.

"What is it?" Heather asked inching closer to Crystal.

"When we were in high school I wanted to sleep with him," Crystal said blushing.

"Did you really?"

"Yes, I did. I thought he was so sexy and bad. He looked so good in those jeans that he wore. I wanted to see what he looked like out of them."

"And now you have. So, are you impressed?" Heather teased.

"I'm very impressed and he still wears his jeans nice and tight," Crystal said licking her lips.

"I always thought he looked nice in his jeans too. He has a nice ass," Heather said with a big grin on her face.

"He is a fine specimen and he's all mine. I just love him," Crystal said.

"I'm so happy for you because everybody is not able to find love," Heather said and squeezed Crystal's hand again.

"I know my brother is the perfect example," Crystal said sitting back down on the bed.

"Why is your brother the perfect example?" Heather asked panicking.

"Don't say anything to him, but we he had his heart broken two years ago and he hasn't recovered from it. He want tell us anything about what happened and he's in a bad mood every day."

"How do you know he had his heart-broken then?" Heather asked getting out of the bed.

"Because some days he'll go off and say things about women and how he loved this woman and she broke his fucking heart. I ask him repeatedly to talk to me and he want. When I find out how this woman is I'm going to kick her ass," Crystal said angrily.

"Why would you do that? I'm sure he'll be all right."

"It's been two years Heather and he's still miserable. My dad is so worried about him, because he wouldn't go out on dates with woman. He said they were all evil and he hated them. So that's why he didn't say anything when he started dating Skyler."

"So, he's better now right?" Heather asked with hope in her eyes. Please, let him be better. The entire Sterner family would hate her if they knew she was the reason for Gabriel's unhappiness and moodiness. They must never know that she slept with Gabe.

"No, he's not better. He doesn't sleep at night and when he does it's a miracle. The other night he finally slept and I heard him snoring and I was so happy he was asleep I went into his room to look at him. He's my little brother and I love him so I look at him sometimes when he sleeps. Then he started to talk and he was saying *please don't leave me, I love you, you were my first come back to me please.* It's just awful and whoever this bitch was she's screwed my brother up."

"I feel so bad," Heather said near tears.

"Heather, it's all right, it's not your fault. Your here on vacation and my brother is not your problem. I'm going to leave now so you can get ready for dinner. Thanks for chatting with me and we still have a lot to talk about. See you in half an hour," Crystal said and left Heather in the room to get ready. Oh my God, what have I done? I've ruined Gabriel's life and his family will hate me forever if he decides to blow the lid off our secret. Something happened when she slept with him. She'd fallen in love with him that's why she'd been celibate for two years. Gabe had ruined it for any other man. She couldn't get him out of her system or the things he said to her. When he called her a slut it had broken her heart and that was another reason she hadn't slept with another man since him. She just focused on her career and she tried her best to stay from men, but Stephen had got her to date him and now they were engaged. He had never tried to get her in bed. He said whenever she was ready all she had to do was let him know. He was so patient with her and she loved him for that, but she wasn't in love with him. She was in love with a man she knew she could never have. How Gabe must hate me? She thought to herself. She got out of the bed and jumped in the shower. She decided to wear a yellow sundress to dinner. She was sitting at the vanity doing her hair when someone knocked on the door.

"Come in," she said.

"I just wanted to let you know that dinner is about to be served," Gabriel said from the doorway.

"Thank you for letting me know Gabe," she said and turned to look at him. He was about to leave and he stopped when she turned around and looked at him. She took his breath away and he almost stumbled. For several moments they just stared at each other. She was the most beautiful woman in the world to him. Damn her for ruining his life, but he still wanted her. He loved her so much it hurt. He wanted so badly to take her into his arms and kiss her passionately.

"I'll see you downstairs Heather and by the way Skyler will be joining us," he said and left the room. Why did he have to be so handsome? Heather thought to herself. How could she sit at the table with him and not touch that face? Why were Mr. and Mrs. Sterner allowing Skyler to come to the dinner for her? Maybe because their son was miserable and they would do anything to make him happy. It was all her fault he was miserable and she deserved to have her rival across the table from her sitting by the man she loved.

Chapter Four

Heather finished getting dressed and went down to dinner. The woman she despised most in the world was kissing the man she loved. She wanted to run back upstairs and weep, but she held her ground and interrupted them, "Hello Skyler."

"Hello Supermodel," Skyler said sarcastically when she pulled away from Gabe.

"I guess you're doing well for yourself. What do you do now? Are you a professional escort yet?" Heather asked nastily.

"Why you high class bitch…"

"Ladies please stop it," Gabe said getting up from the couch.

"I will not stop. She comes in here thinking she's better than me because she's some top model. Well, let me tell you something…"

"You stop right there young lady," Lewis Sterner said coming into the room, "If you disrespect my Heather I'll have to ask you to leave my house."

"But Mr. Sterner, she started," Skyler pouted.

"I don't care who started it, you will not disrespect any

of my girls. Do you understand?" Lewis snapped cutting Skyler off.

"Yes, I understand and I know where I stand in this house," Skyler said and stomped into the dining room.

"Oh, Heather, Ricky said he'll be here very shortly," Lewis said and returned to dining area.

"I guess Mr. Wonderful is running a little late," Gabe said to Heather.

"Yeah, I guess so," Heather said and pulled her hair back into place that fell from the ponytail.

"Let me see your hand again," Gabriel said and took her hand before she could resist, "Are you engaged?"

"Not exactly," she said pulling her hand away.

"What the hell does that mean?" he asked angrily.

"I don't want to talk about it."

"Why the hell not Heather?"

"I just don't want to, okay," she said and started walking towards the dining room. Gabriel ran after her and grabbed her arm.

"Are you already married?" he asked.

"No, I am not already married and the ring is a promise ring. Are you happy now?"

"No, I'm furious, because you're going to marry another man and you know I'm madly in love with you," he said in a low growl. Heather stared at him and before she could speak Ricky walked in.

"Wow! Heather you look gorgeous! Are you ready for dinner?" he asked happily and held his arm out for her to hold.

"Yes, I'm starved Ricky. You look very handsome by the way," Heather said grateful that he walked in. They made their way to the dining room table.

"Heather, you and Ricky look so cute together," Crystal said and earned a scowl from her brother who walked in right behind them. Everyone was at the table so Marie stood up and made a toast to Heather.

"Heather, you're like a daughter to me and I just wanted to take this opportunity to let you know how much we all love you and let you know that we're so glad that you're here to visit us. You'll always have a place here and I'm really glad you're home. This is your home and I love you. To Heather, my second daughter."

"Oh, Mom, thank you so much for that beautiful speech," Heather said near tears. She'd been calling Marie Sterner mom for several years.

"Heather, stand up and give a speech," Crystal said.

"Yeah, Heather, since everybody loves you so much because you're so wonderful let them know how grateful you are," Gabe said speaking for the first time.

"Oh no," Skyler said.

"Watch your mouth young lady," Lewis said.

"Go on Heather, give us a speech," Ricky said. Heather got out her chair and looked around at the face of the people she loved. Then she saw two faces that were giving her menacing looks. She decided to focus on Lewis, Marie, Crystal, and Ricky.

"I just want to start off by saying thank you so much to

the Sterner's for always being there for me. Mr. and Mrs. Sterner you're the parents I've always wanted. You came to all my events and all basketball games. I love you guys so much. Crystal, my best friend in the entire world that I trust with my life; you're the sister I've always wanted. I can't imagine my life without you guys in it. You mean the world to me and I hope that you'll love me always no matter what. Gabriel I just want to say that I love you very much. Ricky, my first love, thank you for being here to welcome me back; you'll always have a special place in my heart. You taught me how to love and I'll be grateful to you for that," Heather said and sat back down.

"Heather, that was beautiful," Marie said with tears in her eyes.

"Yes, Heather that was very beautiful and I love you like a sister too," Crystal said and got out of her chair and came around and gave her a big hug.

"Crystal you're going to make me cry again," Heather said near tears again.

"Can we eat all ready?" Skyler said but was ignored by everyone.

"Heather, I noticed a ring on your finger. Are you engaged?" Lewis asked. He earned a hard stare from Gabriel.

"No, dad it's a promise ring. I promised the guy that I'm dating that I'd think about his proposal to me. Before you ask his name is Stephen Daniels and we've been dating for two years. He's a very smart man and he has an MBA from Harvard. He's 28 years old he has no kids and he's never been married. He's absolutely wonderful and I really like him. He's the CEO of the largest company in New York. I met him when I did a photo-shot in the Caribbean. He was on vacation and he asked me out when we met at a club and we've been dating ever since. He's supposed to fly in a couple of days to come and meet you guys. He may not be able to make it because of his schedule, but he's going to try his best to get here and meet you guys."

"He sounds wonderful dear I'm sure we'll love him," Marie said.

"If he's so wonderful why haven't you accepted his proposal?" Gabriel asked with a menacing look on his face.

"Gabriel, that's none of your concern," Lewis said to his son and gave him a scowled look.

"I'm curious to Supermodel. Do you still need time to screw other men?" Skyler asked nastily.

"That's it Skyler, I want you out of my house now," Marie Sterner said.

"If she leaves I leave," Gabriel said to his mother jumping out of his seat.

"That's fine by me son, but if you want to be seen around town with that so be it. I hope you know I'm very disappointed in you. Why would you choose to date someone that obviously hates someone that we love very much?" Marie said to her son with sadness in her eyes.

"Alright I'll stay. Skyler, I'll see you around," he said and sat back in his seat.

"I was bored with this anyway. Call me when you're ready for you know what," she said and kissed him right on the mouth and left from the room.

"I'm so happy that's she's gone," Lewis said.

"I'm happy too we've never liked each other much," Heather said more to herself than for everyone else.

"That's because you were both screwing Mr. Wonderful over here at the same time," Gabriel said flippantly.

"Don't you dare talk to her that way?" Ricky said angrily.

"Excuse me, I'm not hungry anymore," Heather said and ran from the room.

"Gabriel, I don't know what's you, but if you ever disrespect my best friend like that you'll find yourself without someone to call your sister," Crystal said and rose from her seat.

"Crystal, please sit back down. I'll go apologize to her. I had no right to talk to her like that," Gabriel said and went after Heather.

"Wow! What has gotten into him?" Ricky said.

"We have no idea, but we wish we knew," Marie Sterner said shaking her head.

Chapter Five

Heather was lying on the bed when Gabriel entered her room. She looked absolutely stunning and he would've given his right arm to kiss her at that moment. She wasn't crying, but she looked very sad.

"Are you all right?" Gabriel said walking towards the bed.

"How long have you been sleeping with her?"

"What?" Gabriel said caught off guard by her question.

"You heard me Gabe. Why are you sleeping with her? You know she hates me," Heather said with her face still in a pillow.

"I don't have to answer that. I just wanted to apologize for what I said earlier. I had no right to say that especially in front of my parents. They don't need to know you were a slut in high school. Even though I'm pretty sure they heard rumors about you too."

"Is that you're apology?" Heather asked bringing her face from the pillow.

"That's all you're going to get from me. They all think you're a perfect little angel at that dinner table. You have them fooled real good. You should pat yourself on the back Supermodel. They have no idea you're the one who turned me my life upside down. What would they think of you then?" He asked grabbing her face with both hands, "What would my parents think of you if they found out you fucked my brains on the night of my college graduation and then left me alone?

"Gabe, please stop it. I told you I was sorry and it should've happened. Please forgive me." Heather said near sobs.

"How can I Heather? You've haunted my dreams for two years and I can't get you out of my head. I've almost gone completely insane over you and you want me to forgive you. You knew I was in love with you and you still slept with me and then you left me. Why did you do that to me? Why damn it why?" Gabriel yelled. Before she could answer Crystal walked in.

"Gabriel, why are you yelling at her?" Crystal demanded.

"He wasn't yelling at me. He was just trying to make laugh and come back down to dinner," Heather said with tears still in her eyes.

"Are you okay Heather?" Crystal asked with concern.

"I'm fine you guys do back to dinner and I'll be there in two minutes.

"All right. See you downstairs then," Crystal said and kissed Heather on the cheek and then she left the room. Gabe was right behind her.

"Gabe wait," She called after him.

"What is it?"

"Earlier you said you haven't slept with another woman in two years. Was that true? Or was that lie? Are you really sleeping with Skyler?" Heather asked not expecting an answer from him.

"Not that it's any of your business, but I've never slept with Skyler. I'm still hurting from what you did to me."

"Gabe, I'm sorry for the pain I've caused you. What will it take for you to forgive me?"

"Make love with again tonight when everyone has fallen asleep and I'll forgive you."

"You can't be serious. I have a fiancé and I can't do that to him," Heather said in a soft whisper

"You said he wasn't your fiancé just yet," Gabe said and grabbed her by the arm.

"He's not, but I can't cheat on him; he trusts me too much. It would crush him if he found out."

"Don't make me beg you Heather. I need you and I know that will make me better. I need to make love you again to ensure myself that you were only a childhood crush and when we made the first time I only thought I loved you because I thought I did because of my childhood crush. Please let me make love you again just once more. It will prove that I'm not really in love with you," he said and released her arm.

"All right tonight after everyone is asleep come over to my room and make love with me all night. I'll leave the door unlocked and I'll be waiting for you and when I say make love all night I mean all night." Heather said licking her lips.

"I can't wait," Gabe said and left the room. Five minutes later Heather returned to dinner.

"Are you all right dear?" Marie Sterner asked.

"I feel much better. Gabe apologized to me and we made up," Heather said gazing at Gabe.

"Yes, mother I apologized to her and we're friends again. I'm sure we'll be getting along pretty good after tonight," Gabriel said gazing back at Heather.

"Well, I'm glad you came back down Heather," Ricky said and squeezed her hand.

"Thank you for saying that," Heather said to Ricky and kissed his cheek.

"Oh, please stop kissing at the table," Gabriel said annoyed.

"I'm sorry I want kiss anyone else at the table if it annoys you Gabe," Heather said as she got up and kissed Gabriel right on the mouth. He blushed until he was bright red.

"It's okay if you kiss me anytime," Gabriel said blushing harder.

"Is that so?" Heather said kissing him again on the mouth and then she went back to her seat.

"Why Gabriel Sterner, I haven't seen you blush in years. Will you look at that Lewis?" Marie Sterner said happily.

"Not only is he blushing mom, he's also smiling," Crystal said happily then she turned to Heather and whispered," He still has a major crush on you. I think he's half way in love with you."

"Heather, you should've come to visit sooner," Lewis said happily.

"Yeah, Heather my son hasn't been happy in a while. You're the first person to make him smile in a long time," Marie said.

"I knew your being here would cheer him up," Crystal said.

"Can we eat now? I'm starving," Ricky said.

"Of course we can and we're going to have champagne. Suzy bring in the main course please," Lewis Sterner said to the maid.

Everybody was so happy during dinner and they talked about everything. Even Gabriel and Ricky had a nice conversation. The Sterner's talked to Heather about her modeling career. Heather looked up and Gabe was staring at her. He mouthed to her that he'd be in her room at midnight, so she better get be ready for a hard ride. Heather nearly choked on her food and Ricky handed her his class of water.

"Thank you so much Ricky. You're still the sweetest man I've ever know. I'll always have a special place for you in my heart."

"You take my breath away still after all these years. Let's go outside and talk for a little while," he said getting up from his chair.

"Alright. If you guys will excuse us we're going to go outside and take a walk," Heather said as Ricky helped her up from her chair. Heather heard Gabriel mumble something under his breath as they walked past him. They walked all around the yard and they talked about everything. Heather remembered why she loved him when she was younger. Besides being sinfully handsome he was the most caring man in the world. He had wonderful manners and he treated her like a princess. He looked like had just stepped out of a magazine and into the yard.

"Why don't you model?" Heather asked him.

"Who me?"

"Yes, you silly. You're the most attractive man I've ever known and I don't think you realize how gorgeous you are," she said and kissed his cheek.

"Stop, now you're making me blush. I can't believe you made tough guy Gabe blush like that. That was pretty funny. Anyway, I've never been interested in modeling. I hate having my photograph taken and I refuse to lie around half-naked while somebody takes pictures of me. Then have my pictures plastered all over billboards and magazines for people to see at anytime. I don't think so."

"Well, I see how you feel about my profession. By the way you look damn good half-naked and completely naked." Heather said with a grin on her face making him blush.

"Thanks for saying that. I always wanted to know what you thought about my naked body," Ricky joked.

"It was the best body I'd ever seen at the time," she teased.

"Back to the modeling, I just meant that modeling is not for me. I totally respect what you do. You're a beautiful woman and you're a great model. I have all you're pictures and I have five copies of your first magazine cover. I'm your biggest fan," he said and this time she blushed.

"We were good together and I'm glad that you I have you in my life. Thank you for always being there when I needed you. Do you remember when I called you at 3am when I got my first photo-shoot?"

"Yes, and you scared the hell out if me. I thought something was wrong because you were calling so late and you hadn't called me in three months. I was so happy for you and I felt special that you called me. We'll always be friends right?"

"Right on Ricky. Did you know that you were my first?" She said asked shyly.

"What?" He stammered.

"You were my first and I'll never forget you," she said.

"Wow! I can't believe that. I was supermodel's Heather first lover. I feel damn good about that and not because you're a supermodel, but because it's you," he said and hugged her tight, "I'll always love you tree-top."

"You haven't called me that in years," Heather said very close to tears.

"I know. You were the tallest girl in the entire school. You had supermodel written all over you since age twelve. You were 5'7 at age what age?"

"I think I was twelve and I was 5'7 and I weighed about 100. I was so skinny and I hated it. I'm still skinny, but I have a few curves. I haven't grown since I was fifteen," Heather said.

"How tall are you now?" Ricky said pulling her hair.

"I'm five ten and I love it. We should get back before they wonder what we're doing," before Gabe wonders what we're doing.

"I have to go it's getting late and I have to work in the morning. Can you believe it's already 11:15? I'll come visit you in a couple of days and I want you to meet my girlfriend," Ricky said as they were walking back towards the house.

"I hope it's not somebody I'll dislike," Heather said teasing him.

"I'm sure you'll like her a lot. I really like her and you're opinion means a lot to me so tell me how you really feel after you meet her. I know I shouldn't do this but I compare all my girlfriends to you," he said blushing again.

"That's very flattering; but stop that please. If you like her keep her no matter what I think," Heather said as they arrived back at the house.

"I'll try. I'll see you tomorrow cover girl. Slap Gabe on the head for me and kiss that beautiful best friend of yours on the mouth for me," Ricky said and headed down the drive. She waved good-bye to him as he drove away and then she headed in the house. Crystal was waiting for her on the couch.

"Great, you're back Heather. Come sit by me," Crystal said patting a spot next to her. Heather walked over and sat by her and kissed her smack on the mouth, "Wow! What was that for?" Crystal said blushing.

"You're the third person I've made blush today. That was from Ricky. He asked me to kiss my beautiful best friend on the mouth."

"Thanks, I guess. I just wanted to know if you would be okay if I went on a date tonight."

"You mean you're going to get laid. Nobody has a date this late unless it's hot sex. Of course I'm not going to stop you from having hot sex. Go get it girl," Heather said giving her friend a sly smile.

"I feel so bad though because you just arrived today and I'm going on a date and I'm going to have sex and you haven't had sex in two years."

"Please, don't remind me," but you want be the only one getting lucky.

"I'm leaving shortly. I just have to freshen up, but I'll see you at breakfast in the morning. Maybe," she said happily and went upstairs. Heather looked at the clock and it was 11:30. She headed upstairs and prepared herself for Gabriel Sterner.

She sprayed perfume behind her ears and on her wrist. She had chosen to wear her sexiest nightgown. It was Gabriel's favorite color red. She knew it would drive him wild. She decided not to light candles just in case someone walked by during the night they wouldn't be suspicious by the light. She was going towards her bed and she heard a lit knock on the door. Her heart jumped to her throat and he pulse quickened. She opened the door and Gabriel grabbed her by the waist and crushed his mouth to hers. He made love to her mouth until they were both breathless. He picked her up and carried her to the bed. He devoured her mouth again until she could barely breathe. He put a finger on her mouth and whispered, "Don't talk just enjoy," and then he crushed his mouth to hers again. Then he gently took her nightgown off and placed soft kisses all over her body. Heather felt as if she was floating and she never wanted to come down. Gabriel placed his hand on her center and she was moist for him. He slipped a finger inside of her and she went over the edge. She tried to cry out his name, but he devoured her mouth once again. He replaced his finger with his mouth and he feasted on her middle until she went over the edge a second time. She grabbed handfuls of his hair and panted out his name. Gabriel thought he would explode right then. He came up and kissed her on the mouth and then he entered her. She was tight like a glove and he wanted to release himself inside of her, but he slowed his pace and she went over the edge again and he followed soon after. Afterwards they were in complete silence. Neither had any idea what to say to the other. Gabe got up and was about to leave the bed and Heather grabbed his arm and said, "Please stay the night," he answered by devouring her mouth and slipping inside of her again.

Chapter Six

The next morning when Heather awoke she was alone. There was a note on Gabe's pillow and it read *I know my answer now and you were great. Thank you for making love to me again for the last time. You're fiancé will be proud to have a woman like you in his bed for the rest of his life.* What did the note mean? Heather thought to herself. She got out of bed and she felt sore and incredibly limber from all the lovemaking she and Gabriel had. He was such an incredible lover and he had amazing hands. She wanted those hands on her body again. Just the thought of him touching her again made her weak in the knees. She had to stop thinking about Gabe she told herself. She went into the bathroom and got ready for the day. While she was in the shower she kept having flashbacks of the night before with Gabe. He was so amazing and she knew it could never happen again. What if he doesn't love me anymore she thought to herself? He said he knows his answer now and that I was great and he was glad that he had me one last time. It's obvious that it was just a childhood crush that went on to long and he never really loved me. Heather thought to herself and started to cry. Twenty minutes later she went downstairs to have breakfast with the Sterner family.

"Heather, Mr. and Mrs. Sterner and Crystal will not be joining you this morning. It will just be you and Gabriel," the cook said.

"Why not? Is something wrong?" Heather asked with concern.

"Mr. and Mrs. Sterner had to go into town to visit an ill friend and Miss Crystal came in late last night and she is still sleeping. Gabriel will be down shortly. The Sterner's asked me to make sure you knew why they would not be here. Breakfast will be served in five minutes. Would you like some coffee before you eat?"

"No, thank you and thanks for the messages," Heather said. Right after the cook left Gabriel entered the room with a very big smile on his face.

"Good morning Heather. Did you sleep well last night?" he asked sitting directly across from her.

"Yes, I slept very well, what about you?" she said not looking in his eyes.

"I slept like a baby. I feel very good this morning. My head isn't cloudy anymore and I can't remember the last time I was this happy."

"I know you're family will be happy that you're in a good mood and you're happy again. You look very handsome when you smile Gabe you should do it more often," Heather said to him.

"I think I'll be smiling a lot more. I just feel so good and

I think I'm going to be happy from now on. Would you like to go to dinner with me tonight and then make love afterwards?" he asked without blinking his eyes.

"What?" Heather stammered. Before he could reply the maid walked in with the breakfast trays.

"Here Gabriel, your breakfast just the way you like it," she said happily.

"Thank you Suzy," he said.

"No problem Gabriel, anything for you," Suzy said blushing and then she left the room.

"Wow! Has she got the hots for you?" Heather said.

"She does not, she just thinks I'm really cute and she wants me to take her to bed," Gabriel said evenly.

"Gabriel what you said earlier...."

"Good morning you two; sorry I'm late for breakfast," Crystal said when she came into the room glowing.

"Good morning sister late night last night?" Gabriel asked getting up from his chair and kissing his sister in the cheek. She just looked at him with surprise in her eyes, "What?" He asked.

"I can't remember the last time you were nice to me. Are you all right?" she asked sitting down next to Heather.

"I'm fine. I'm just in a good mood this morning," he said happily.

"I see I'm not the only one who got lucky last night," she joked to Gabriel and Heather almost choked on her food, "Are you all right," Crystal asked.

"Yes, I'm fine my food went down the wrong pipe," Heather managed to choke out.

"Gabriel, what has made you so happy? Please don't tell me you slept with Skyler? You're happiness answers the question for me. At least your happy little brother," Crystal said.

"I am happy and I did get laid real good last night. I want say anything else about it because I don't want to spoil your appetite big sister. But I will say this it was incredible and I want to have her again and again. It was even better than the first time we did it and I thought that was the best it could ever be. How's your breakfast Heather?" he asked looking her in the eyes and making her melt in the inside.

"Everything is fine Gabe. I guess your date was great last night Crystal. Make sure you give me all the details later," Heather said turning her attention away from Gabe.

"You know I will. What did you do last night?" Crystal asked Heather.

"Yeah, Heather, what did you do last night?" Gabriel asked with a big grin on his face. Before she could answer Suzy came in and said, "Heather, there's a Stephen Daniels on the phone for you."

"Thank you so much Suzy. Excuse me please you guys. I'll be back after I take this call," Heather said not looking into Gabe's menacing face.

"Hi Stephen, I'm so glad to hear your voice. I miss you to sweetheart. When can you come in? In two days that's great. Everything is fine here and I can't wait to see you.

I told the Sterner's all about you and they can't wait to meet you. I'll see you in two days. Love you Stephen." She said and hung up the phone. She leaned against the wall and gathered her thoughts and then she returned to the table to finish her breakfast.

"How's Stephen doing?" Crystal asked.

"He's great and he's going to be flying in; in two days. He's very excited about meeting you guys. I can't wait for you to meet him. He's so wonderful," Heather said.

"Is he really Heather?" Gabe asked giving her hard stare.

"Of course he is," Heather said looking away from his gaze.

"That's great Heather and I know we'll all like him," Crystal said squeezing her hand.

"He's very excited about meeting you guys. I need to go into town and get my hair and nails before he gets here. I like to look my best for him. I also need a facial. Crystal you'll have to take to were you get everything done for yourself."

"Sure thing supermodel. We can go when we finish breakfast. I think I'll get my hair and nails done to. Gabe would you like you to join us out on the town today?" Crystal asked happily.

"I really don't think I'd feel comfortable at a beauty salon all day. Besides I don't want to see, never mind. I'm going to my room now. Have a good time," Gabriel said and left from the table.

"Gabriel, wait," Heather said and went after him. She turned to Crystal and said, "I'll be right back," She caught up with Gabe as he was walking up the stairs. She grabbed him by the arm and made him stop walking.

"Let me go Heather before I kiss you and take you to bed again."

"I'd love for you to take me to bed," Heather said out-loud not meaning to.

"Damn it, why did you say that?" Gabe asked when he let her go and turned away from her, "You were so damn good in bed. I loved the feel of you underneath me."

"Gabe, please lower your voice before someone hears you," Heather hissed at him.

"So, what if they hear we slept together? They're going to hear when your fiancé comes and you fuck him," Gabriel growled at her.

"Gabriel, please don't say things like that to me," Heather said almost sobbing.

"How dare you talk about preparing yourself for another man right after you had me? My scent is still all over you and your all ready making plans to be with another man. Have you even changed your sheets yet? Can you still feel me inside of you? You may be a top supermodel, but you're still a slut," Gabriel said as he snatched his arm away from her and headed back upstairs. Heather ran to the bathroom and washed her face. Then she went back down to breakfast with her best friend.

"What time would you like to leave?" Crystal asked Heather when she sat down.

"I'd like to leave right now if you don't mind. I haven't been here in so long and I'd like to see how everything looks now."

"Well, just let me brush my teeth and we can go. Are you all right Heather? You look kind of pale," Crystal said when she got out of her chair.

"I'm fine I'm just ready to get outside and get some fresh air. I'll meet you outside by the car," Heather said as she got out of her chair. She kissed her best friends forehead and left the room.

Chapter Seven

Upstairs Gabriel Sterner was fired up. He knew after what happened last night he was done for. He wanted her again already. He could've choked her when she sat at that table and said how she liked to look good for Mr. Perfect and how she had to go get her hair and nails done. Damn her. She looked so beautiful this morning when she was sitting at the table. He could've eaten her alive. He knew now that she wasn't a child hood crush and he wanted her to be is wife. He was head over heels in love with her and she was to be married to another man. He would surely die if she married this Stephen Daniels guy. He knew he'd go insane when Stephen came to visit and he shared the room with his Heather right next door. What if he heard them making love? He would kill them both.

"I have to get out of her before he arrives," Gabriel said. He grabbed his car keys and headed for the door. He made it to his car and he saw Heather sitting under a tree nearby. He wanted to ignore her, but she looked so sad and alone. He walked over to her and touched her shoulder.

"I guess the test came back negative," she asked flippantly

"What?" he asked sitting down by her.

"Remember when we slept together the first time and you called me a slut."

"I didn't mean that," Gabriel said holding his head down.

"Well, you called me that again I was convinced this time that you meant it. I thought to myself why would he sleep with me if he thought I was a disgusting slut. Then I realized the test must have come back negative. You must really like whores why else would you date Skyler?"

"Heather, I didn't mean it when I called you a slut. I'm a jealous fool and I want you for myself. Please, don't marry this guy. I want to make love to you and only you for the rest of our lives. I realized last night that I love you more than ever. I want you to marry me and have my children," Gabriel said almost pleading.

"How dare you say that to me? Do you really think after you called me a slut I'm going to sleep with you again? Do you have any idea how bad you hurt me when you called me that? I will never sleep with you again after that." Heather said looking into his eyes.

"Heather, please forgive me for what I said. I didn't mean it I was upset," Gabriel said grabbing her hand.

"I will never forgive you for what you said. After last night I thought we could have something special, but I was wrong. I saw you're note and I had no idea what it meant, but you made it pretty clear when you expressed you're disgust for me. Last night was beautiful, but we will never make love again. I have to go now I see your sister coming over. By the way if you think I'm a slut now, wait until Stephen comes and you hear me screaming his name threw the walls," Heather said nastily as she got up, "You may want to get some ear plugs to block out all of the screaming," Then she left him sitting by the tree with a look of disbelief on his face.

"Heather, why does my brother have that look on his face?" Crystal said to Heather as she got into the car.

"How should I know what's going on with your cruel brother? Let's go and I want to have a cocktail later, but I also want a massage. By the way everything is on me today," Heather said.

"Wow! I feel so special; can I get any hair-do I want?" Crystal asked excitedly.

"Of course you can and you're getting you a massage, facial, manicure, and a pedicure beautiful. You need to look you're best next time you see Kenneth. When is he coming over to meet everybody?" Heather said.

"I'm not sure because I don't think daddy approves of me dating him. Daddy has never liked Kenneth and he knows we're sleeping together so he really hates him now. I'm crazy about him though. He's such a good lover and we have another date tonight and I can't wait to have him again," Crystal said as they drove out of the yard.

"He must be damn good in bed. When you came to the

table this morning you were glowing like a candle. I'm so happy for you Crystal. How does he feel about you?" Heather asked.

"I don't know Heather. I haven't told him that I love him, but I want to every time we make love. Lately it seems that all we do now is make love. We never go out anymore and it bothers me. I'm starting to think he's just using me for sex. The other day I heard a woman say that she had amazing sex with a man named Kenneth," Crystal said sounding sad.

"That doesn't mean it was your Kenneth and don't jump to conclusions. Has he ever given you any reason not to trust him?"

"No, but we never go out during the day and we always eat dinner out of town like he's trying to make sure we're not seen by anybody we know. I don't like that and I think that maybe I should stop seeing him," Crystal said.

"Just talk to him before you just break off the relationship. You said that you love him and you shouldn't break up with him without telling him why. He makes you happy and I know it because I saw how you were glowing this morning. If he makes you happy you stay with him. Get all the facts before you judge him Crystal," Heather said angrily.

"All right I'm sorry calm down please. I'll talk to him first before I make a decision. I'm so in love with him and I'm not going to let him go so easily," Crystal said on good spirits.

"That's my girl. You make sure after you talk to him you tell me everything," Heather said. They drove the rest of the way in silence. Heather was thinking about her argument with Gabe. Does he really want to marry me? How would the Sterner's react if she and Gabe got engaged? Would they be happy or would they say it would never work?

Chapter Eight

"Earth to Heather," Crystal said grabbing Heather by her arm, "What are you thinking about? You were a million miles away."

"I'm sorry I was day dreaming. What did you ask me?" Heather said coming out of her daze.

"We're at the beauty salon. You can get out now supermodel. You get to skip everybody; because you're famous and since I'm your best friend I get to skip everybody too," Crystal said happily. Heather and Crystal got out of the car and headed into the salon. Everybody was in awe of Heather's beauty. They just gazed at her and said nothing. A woman with spiky yellow hair walked over to Heather and Crystal and said, "Right this way please," Heather and Crystal followed the lady into a beautiful room filled with candles and light classical music was playing in the background. Two more women entered the room and started setting up the materials. Five minutes later Heather and Crystal were being pampered from head to toe. They were receiving scalp massages, manicures, and pedicures.

"Wow! This feels great," Heather said.

"It almost feels better than sex," Crystal purred.

"Almost, but not quite," Heather laughed.

"Especially not the sex I had last night," Crystal said grinning.

"I haven't had a massage in about three weeks. This is just awesome," Heather moaned.

"So, tell me about what's been going in your life these past few years," Crystal said to her best friend.

"Wow! There's so much to tell I don't know where to start," Heather said with a sad face.

"Are you thinking about you parents?" Crystal asked.

"Yes, I really miss them and I wish I could just have five minutes to see them just one last time. My dad would be so proud of me for making something for myself. He was such a wonderful dad and so supportive of me. I carry a picture of him in my wallet for good luck," Heather said near tears.

"Heather, that's so sweet. I don't want you to be sad, so let's not talk about the past," Crystal said reaching over to squeeze her best friend's hand.

"It's all right, I can talk about them. Well, maybe another time I will. I'll tell you about my modeling and my traveling and my schooling," Heather said.

"Sounds great," Crystal replied.

They left three hours later floating on cloud nine. Then they headed to the "After Wall" for cocktails. When they sat down at a booth, a pair of eyes watched them. Kenneth Elliot watched his beautiful lover as she talked to her supermodel best friend at their booth. She was beautiful and she was all his. He couldn't believe he was dating Crystal Sterner and he was sleeping with her. He never thought he would have gotten her to date him, much less in bed with him. And she was amazing. And you were a damn virgin. He continued to watch her as she talked with her best friend. She took his breath away. He remembered when they were in high school and how she never wanted attention to be drawn to her. She was very quiet and sweet and her best friend was the complete opposite and no one could understand why they were friends. Crystal's family was filthy rich and Heather's family was barely getting by, but the Sterner family embraced Heather with open arms and little Gabe fell in love with her. Most people would've probably thought Heather would end up with a guy like him and not her sweet and quiet best friend. No one even really knew they were dating. Crystal said she would tell her parents about him soon and he was okay with that. As long as he could have her that's all that mattered. He was obsessed with her and he had been since they were in high school.

"Hey Heather, I see Kenneth at the bar. I'm going to go over and say hi and ask him to come over," Crystal said and left the table. They locked eyes and Crystal walked over to him. Their faces were filled with love for one another.

"Hi gorgeous," he asked before he kissed her passionately on the mouth.

"Hi, I'm here with my best friend Heather. Do you remember her?" she asked.

"Of course I do. I'll come over and have a drink with you guys. Would you like that?" Kenneth said standing up and grabbing her by the waist. He whispered something inappropriate in her ear and made her blush.

"Kenneth, I need to talk to you in private before we go to the table," Crystal said seriously.

"All right, let's go in the back and talk," Kenneth said guiding her to the back of the restaurant. They found a table and sat down.

"Are you sleeping with other women?" Crystal asked harshly.

"Where did you get that from?" he asked angrily.

"Why are you ashamed to take me to restaurants in town and why don't you take me out like you use to?" Crystal hissed at him.

"Is that what this is about? Because I keep you in bed all the time and we go to restaurants thirty minutes away I'm sleeping with other woman?" Kenneth asked jumping out of his chair.

"I heard a woman say the other day that she slept with you. When did you have time to take her to bed? Did you take her to your place or did you use our special place," Crystal asked with venom in her mouth.

"I keep you in bed all the time because you're the best lover I've ever had and for your information I take you to restaurants out of town because their nicer than the ones here and I think you deserve the best. I can't believe you don't trust me. I've never given you any reason not to trust me. This relationship is over. Good-bye Crystal you were great," Kenneth said and stomped away from her.

"Kenneth, wait give me another chance," Crystal cried after him. He stopped in his tracks and turned around.

"Why should I Crystal?" he said threw gritted teeth.

"Because I'm in love with you and I want to be with you for the rest of my life," Crystal said with tears running down her eyes. Kenneth was speechless by the words Crystal spoke to him.

"What did you say?" He asked in an emotional voice.

"I'm in love with you and I have been for a while now," Crystal sobbed.

"Why didn't you tell me when you first fell in love with me?" he asked.

"I didn't know if you loved me in return," Crystal managed to choke out. Kenneth walked over to her and took her in his arms.

"I love you too baby," Kenneth said.

"Do you really, Kenneth?" Crystal asked with hope in her eyes.

"Of course I do. I have since we were in high school," Kenneth said kissing her on the mouth.

"I had no idea Kenneth. Why didn't you say something to me back then?"

"I didn't think you'd care," Kenneth said turning his back on her.

"I had a little crush on you when we were in high school. I wanted to go to bed with you," Crystal said blushing.

"Did you really?" He asked

"Yes, I did. I knew you'd be real good in bed and I was right," Crystal said and kissed him on the mouth.

"I wanted to sleep with you too, but I didn't think you'd give me the time of day. I never thought you'd care to talk to me," he said

"Well, I care now and I'm glad that we have one another," Crystal said wrapping her arms around his waist from the back.

"Let's go back to the table before Heather thinks we bailed on her," he said as he led her back to the main room.

"There you are. I was wondering what happened to you guys. Is everything all right?" Heather asked with concern.

"We're fine; thanks for asking," Crystal said as she sat down next to Heather. They heard commotion at the front door and it was Gabriel and Skyler walking in arm in arm.

"Oh no, here comes trouble," Crystal said under her breath.

"What does he see in her? I just don't get it. Waiter, bring me another drink please," Heather said angrily.

"Heather, it's just a phase he's going through. I just hope he's using protection when he sleeps with her. There's no telling where she's been. I'm just glad that he's seeing someone," Crystal said.

"Even if it's Skyler?" Heather asked.

"Yes, even if it's Skyler. You have no idea the shape my brother was in for about two years. It was awful and he wouldn't date anybody. He was like a damn zombie. Whoever the bitch was that broke his heart; really did him over. I'm glad he's finally seeing someone and I don't care if it's Skyler. As long as he's happy that's all that matters. Did you see how happy he was this morning at breakfast? He hasn't smiled in such a long time. If Skyler is the reason for his happiness I'm glad that she's around."

"I guess you're right Crystal," Heather said unhappily and asked the waiter for another drink.

"Are we still on for tonight beautiful?" Kenneth asked.

"Of course we are; I'll see you tonight in about two hours," Crystal said kissing him on the cheek.

"Where are we going to meet baby?" Kenneth asked.

"At my house; I want you to meet my parents again so we can talk. What do you think about that?"

"I don't want to do that tonight. I just want you to myself. I'll pick you up at eight o'clock tonight and we're going to go to a nice restaurant and then you know what is going to follow afterwards. See you them. Nice seeing you again Heather, you look beautiful as always. I'll bring a magazine over sometime this week. Will you sign it for me?" Kenneth asked.

"Of course I will, but you have to promise to be good to my best friend," Heather said.

"I'll never hurt her. She's very special to me," he said as he rose from his seat, kissed Crystal's lips, and left.

"Oh, he's such a hottie. Heather, are you drunk?" Crystal asked almost laughing.

"Yes, I am and I think you should take me home before I embarrass myself," Heather said in a very drunken voice.

"All right let's go; besides I need to find something to wear for my date tonight," Crystal said helping Heather get up from her chair. They were almost to the door and Skyler cut them off, "Will you look at this? The perfect supermodel is drunk. What would the tabloids think of that?"

"Skyler, get out of my way before I knock you over," Heather said angrily.

"I would like to see you do that why you're drunk beauty queen," Skyler said nastily.

"Skyler, leave them alone. Crystal, I'll help get Heather to the car," Gabriel said and walked over to Heather and picked her and started walking towards the car.

"Gabriel, put her down; she's not your business, I am," Skyler said angrily.

"Skyler, don't be jealous. I'll be back in three minutes. Crystal, go to the bar and get a sprite for Ms. Supermodel here."

"Alright, I'll be at the car in a few minutes," Crystal said and left for the bar. Gabriel walked Heather out to the car and she enjoyed every minute of it. He smelled wonderful and she wanted to sink her teeth into his skin.

"You were great in bed last night, can I have you again tonight?" Heather whispered in is ear.

"Heather, you're drunk and you don't know what you're saying."

"Yes, I do and I want you to put your hands all over me and make love to me. Sneak over to my room tonight and make love to me please," she said and kissed him on the neck.

"Heather, stop that before my sister comes out and she's you," Gabriel said angrily.

"Don't you want to make love to me again?"

"Yes, I do and you know it."

"Well, come to my room tonight and you can have me all you want all night," Heather said in a flirty voice. Before Gabriel could answer Crystal arrived with the Sprite and the keys. She unlocked the door and Gabriel put Heather into the car and buckled her in.

"I'll see you at home later sister," Gabriel said.

"No you want; I have a date little brother. I love you Gabriel Sterner. I'll see you in the morning."

"I love you to and I guess I'll see you later than supermodel in a couple of hours."

"You bet your ass you will," Heather said and blew him a kiss and then Crystal drove off.

"You are so drunk," Crystal laughed.

"Why do you say that?" Heather grinned.

"Because it just sounded like you we're making plans to be with my brother later tonight."

"Well, we know that's absurd," Heather said trying to sound joking so her friend wouldn't become suspicious.

When they arrived at the house Heather went upstairs to her room and she stripped off her clothes and jumped in the shower. She got out ten minutes later and dried off.

She fell on the bed and fell asleep instantly. Three hours later she was awaking by a pair of probing hands on her body. She opened her eyes and Gabriel Sterner was over her completely naked and iron hard.

"I've been watching you sleep for one hour and you're absolutely beautiful and I'm completely in love with you. I have to have you Heather," he said and devoured her mouth with his. He made love to her mouth and he took her breath away. He made his way down her body and he slipped his fingers inside of her. She was slippery wet for him and he took her over the edge.

"Let me see you cum baby. Don't hold back from me. Let it go Heather," he whispered and jabbed his tongue inside of her and made her orgasm all most too much to take. She went over the edge and cried out his name. She grabbed handfuls of his hair and panted out his name again.

"Yes, yes, say my name baby," Gabriel said as he slipped inside of her. She was dripping wet like a fountain and Gabriel wanted to ride her like a saddle. He kissed her passionately as he made his pace a little faster. She matched him stroke for stroke. She rolled her hips and she grabbed his buttocks and that made him climax. He rode her fast and hard and she loved every minute of it. Afterwards he held her in his arms and they fell asleep together.

Chapter Nine

Heather woke with a gorgeous man next to her and she knew she had to get him out of her bed before her best friend found him there.

"Gabe you have to get out of here before someone sees you," Heather said getting out of bed gathering his clothes.

"I'm still tired, Heather don't make me leave. Get back in bed with me please. I want you again," Gabriel said pulling the covers off and showing Heather his arousal.

"Gabe, we can't and you know it. Someone could walk by and hear us making love. You have to sneak out of here before everyone wakes up," Heather said turning away from his aroused manhood.

"All right I'll go, but I'll be back again tonight. Unless you have a problem with me coming back?" he said getting out of bed.

"Gabe, we can't sleep together again. I have a fiancé and he'll be here tomorrow. I was drunk last night and this should've never happened. I have to get clean sheets and everything else. Leave now please," Heather said.

"Fine, I'll go, but just remember when you sleep with

him in that bed; that you made love with me in that same bed only days before. I hope that makes you feel good about yourself," Gabriel said as he stormed out of the room. Heather wanted to go after him but she knew she couldn't. But she really wanted to. Could we have something special? Should I chance it, but what about Stephen? I have to let him go. I know I'm never going to marry him. Why am I giving him false hope?

"What a mess I've made of my life," Heather said out loud. She got dressed and then she went downstairs for breakfast.

"Good morning Heather, how are you?" Suzy the maid asked when Heather sat at the table.

"I feel fine; thank you for asking," Heather said feeling awkward because Suzy never spoke to her.

"I bet you feel very relaxed and limber," Suzy said under her breathe.

"Excuse me, what did you say?" Heather asked angrily.

"I didn't say anything," Suzy said in a low voice.

"Yes, you did. I heard you and what did you mean by that?" Heather asked getting out of her seat and grabbing Suzy by the arm.

"I know you slept with Gabe last night," Suzy hissed at her.

"I did not, why would you say that?" Heather asked, letting go of Suzy's arm.

"I heard you making love last night when I got up to go to the restroom," Suzy said angrily.

"You're sadly mistaken. I wasn't the woman he was making love with. It was someone else," Heather lied.

"I heard the noises coming from your room. How do you explain that?" Suzy asked.

"I don't have to explain myself to you," Heather yelled to Suzy.

"But you will have to explain to your fiancé," Suzy said nastily.

"You'd better keep your mouth closed. Do you understand me?" Heather said in a very angry voice as she grabbed Suzy by the wrist.

"Why should I?" Suzy said holding her ground.

"Well, if you don't, you'll find yourself without a job," Heather said with a sinister smile on her face.

"You can't do that," Suzy cried.

"Oh, yes I can and I will if I have too," Heather said.

"Fine, I want tell anyone your dirty little secret. But, you still have to live with it on your conscience that you're screwing two men at the same time in the same bed," Suzy whispered and left the kitchen. Heather started to get up from her chair to go after Suzy but she changed her mind.

"What is wrong with me? I never talk to people that way," Heather said to herself.

"So, how often do you talk to yourself?" Crystal said when she came into the kitchen.

"Oh, hi, I didn't hear you walking in," Heather said nervously.

"You look upset; are you all right?" Crystal asked after she kissed Heather on the cheek.

"I had a rough night, but I'll be alright," Heather said feeling guilty for lying to her best friend again. She had never lied to Crystal before her visit.

"You don't look so well, do you need to lie back down?" Crystal asked with concern.

"Don't worry about me Crystal. I'm fine, sit down so we came have breakfast," Heather said with a false cheerfulness.

"Breakfast is served," Suzy said angrily when she came in with the breakfast tray. She slammed the food down on the table and headed back towards the door.

"Suzy, have you lost your mind?" Crystal asked the maid.

"I'm sorry I didn't mean to do that. I'm not feeling very well this morning."

"I guess something is going around, because Heather isn't feeling well either."

"Why Heather, what's bothering you this morning?" Suzy asked Heather with a smile on her face.

"Nothing you should worry yourself about. How's your job?" Heather asked with a smile on her face.

"May I take the day off?" Suzy asked looking away from Heather.

"Yes, you may take the day off. I hope you feel better," Crystal said.

"I'm sure I'll feel better in a couple of days when the air is clean again," Suzy said and left the room hurriedly.

"What's gotten into her this morning?" Crystal said to herself.

"I'm starved, let's eat this food," Heather said trying to take Crystal thoughts from Suzy.

"Yeah, let's eat beautiful," Crystal said and started eating with Heather.

"How are you doing Crystal?" Heather asked.

"Oh, I feel very good this morning. Thank you for asking. I had a late night rondavu with Kenneth last night. It was awesome," Crystal said with a big smile on her face.

"Oh, you're a bad girl," Heather teased.

"I am not; maybe just a little, but only for Kenneth."

"You guys look so cute together. I think you're going to be together for a very long time."

"Good, I think so too. Hey, when is that fiancé of yours coming in?" Crystal asked excitedly.

"He'll be here in about three or four days. He had to change his flight date from tomorrow to Thursday," Heather said with a little enthusiasm.

"Heather, you don't sound very excited about him coming in. Are you sure you want him to visit?" Crystal asked with concern.

"Yes, I want him to come and see everybody. I need him to hug me and tell me everything is all right. I need him so bad Crystal. I've made a mess of my life and I don't know what to do," Heather said in tears.

"Heather, what's wrong. What's going on with you?" Crystal asked.

"I can't tell you, you'll hate me forever," Heather said in a whisper.

"Heather, I could never hate you. Please, tell me what's going on," Crystal asked with aggravation in her voice.

"What's going in here?" Gabriel asked suspiciously when he came into the kitchen and saw Heather in tears.

"Gabe, can you give us a minute, please?" Crystal asked her brother angrily.

"Heather, what's the matter with you?" Gabe asked grabbing her face into his hands.

"I can't talk about this. I'm going upstairs now," Heather said and ran from the kitchen.

"What did you do to her?" Gabriel asked his sister angrily.

"I didn't do anything to her. She want tell me what's wrong. She did say that if she told me what's going on with her; I'd hate her forever. What did she mean by that?" Crystal asked with confusion in her voice.

"How should I know? She's your best friend; you should know what's going on with her. I guess she has a deep dark secret that's eating her alive and she's feeling very guilty about," Gabriel said to his sister.

"Heather tells me everything; she wouldn't keep a big secret from me," Crystal yelled.

"Everyone has secrets big sister and that best friend of yours has a really big one," Gabriel said with a big smile on his face.

"You know her secret don't you?" Crystal asked her brother.

"I have no idea what you're talking about," Gabriel said.

"Yes, you do and tell me what's going on right now," Crystal yelled.

"Look, I have to go. I have a breakfast date with Skyler this morning. I'll see you later big sister," Gabriel said and kissed his sister on the forehead and left.

"What's going on in this house?" Crystal screamed as she went upstairs.

Chapter Ten

Upstairs Heather was sobbing into her pillow. She knew she would have to tell Stephen that she slept with Gabe. He would probably dump her on her on the spot. She didn't want to tell him after he took that long flight to see her; that she'd been having an affair with her best friend's brother. He would feel very much betrayed, but she had to tell him. He deserved to know the truth. He was such a wonderful man and he didn't deserve to be betrayed by her. How could she ever live with herself after what she did too him? Heather stayed in her room for the next two days. Crystal was very concerned about her, but Heather told her not to worry. Finally, on the third day she got out of bed around eight o'clock that night undisturbed. She got up took a quick shower and snuck out the back door, but before she left out of the back door she grabbed a pair of keys to a car. She went into the garage and tried every door until she hit the jackpot. She got into the car and drove into town. She decided to go to the bar and have a drink. She sat at a table in the hoping to go unnoticed. The waitress noticed her instantly.

"Hey, you're that beautiful supermodel who's the best friend of Crystal's, aren't you?" the waitress asked.

"Yes, I am, but do me a favor and don't tell anyone I'm here," Heather said.

"Sure thing, but can I have you autograph?" the waitress asked excitedly.

"Yes, but after you bring me my drink," Heather said with a smile on her face.

"Coming right up beautiful lady," the waitress squealed and ran off to get Heather's drink.

Heather waited quietly at her table for the waitress to bring her drink. She was suddenly tapped on her shoulder. She turned around and she was looking into the face of a friend.

"Hi, nice to see you," Heather said happily.

"Nice to see you too, may I join you pretty lady?" The visitor asked.

"Of course you can," Heather said patting the seat next to her.

"So, what are you doing her all by yourself?" The visitor asked.

"I needed to get away and I wanted to be by myself. What are you doing here?" Heather asked.

"I come here twice a week with friends from work. I never thought I'd see you here without Crystal. Where's my girl at anyway?" Kenneth asked happily.

"She's at home. She doesn't even know I'm here. I snuck out of the house and I took someone's car," Heather said smiling.

"What a bad girl you are. I always wondered how you

and Crystal became friends. Tell me the story," Kenneth said pulling Heather's hair.

"All right, but let me get my drink first. Would you like one?" Heather asked waitress came over with her drink.

"Yes, I would, thank you very much."

"What would you like?" Heather asked.

"Whatever you're having my lady."

"Okay, I need another apple martinis, please?" Heather said to the waitress when she put her drink in front of her.

"Coming right up, supermodel," The waitress said and left the table with a big smile on her face.

"Wow! How does it feel to be a supermodel?" Kenneth asked smiling at Heather.

"It feels great. I really like being a model. I get to travel a lot and have my photo taken and be on the cover of magazines. I love traveling to exotic islands and having the photo shoots. It is hard work and I have no privacy, but it's the price you pay for fame."

"Is it worth it?" Kenneth asked.

"Yes, it is, because when I grew up I had nothing. My family was dirt poor and my mother mistreated me because I was beautiful and she wasn't. I never went on a vacation until I went to college. Thank God I was smart and I was able to get that scholarship," Heather said looking very sad thinking about her mother.

"I forgot what you won that scholarship for," Kenneth said.

"I didn't even know that you knew that I won a

scholarship," Heather said surprised that he knew about her scholarship.

"Everybody knew about that. What was it for again?" Kenneth asked.

"I won for having the best GPA in all the area high schools," Heather said feeling embarrassed.

"Wow! That's very impressive and you shouldn't be embarrassed when you say it," Kenneth said pulling her hair again.

"Thank you Kenneth; you are a really great guy. You're just what Crystal needs. I still can't believe you guys are a couple," Heather said.

"I can't either. She's so quiet and classy and smart. And look at me; I'm loud and I have no class and I'm not very smart," Kenneth said looking very serious. The waitress arrived with their drinks and sat them down and then she left after winking at them.

"You forgot incredible sexy and handsome," Heather said making him blush," They say opposites attract. Don't be so hard on yourself. If you didn't deserve Crystal, you wouldn't be with her."

"I guess you're right. I've had a crush on her since we were in high school," Kenneth said blushing again.

"Really, I had no idea. That's so cute. You guys we meant to be together," Heather said kissing him on the cheek.

"Do you really think we make a nice couple?" Kenneth asked.

"Yes, I do and I think you guys should get married," Heather said.

"Okay, on that note, let's dance," Kenneth said and pulled Heather to the dance floor.

"I use to dance with my dad to this song at home all the time when I was little. It was his favorite song of all time," Heather replied and a single tear rolled down her cheek.

"Are you all right?" Kenneth asked wiping her tears away.

"Yes, I'm fine. I just miss my parents sometime. My mother passed away right after I won that scholarship. She apologized to me on her death bed for the way she treated me and then she just died. My father was devastated because her death was so sudden. My mother was never ill and suddenly she got sick and she died three days later."

"Heather, I had no idea how your mother died. I'm so sorry," Kenneth said.

"I've never told anybody, not even Crystal. I miss my mother so much. My father adored my mother and he died the day after I left for college. I think he was holding on long enough to see me to go off to college. I'm sorry for talking your ear off," Heather said breaking away. She walked back to the table and ordered another drink.

"Heather, are you all right?" Kenneth asked when he made it back to the table.

"I'll be all right. Thank you for letting me get that out. Hey, I didn't tell you how Crystal and I became friends."

"I completely forgot about that," Kenneth said happy Heather was cheering up again.

"Well, when we were in the fifth grade there was this big contest between the girls. It wasn't a real contest, but it was a big deal for the girls. It was to see who the prettiest girl was in fifth grade. It just happened to be on a Friday and I had on my new dress my dad had gotten for me. Every Thursday my dad would bring me home a new dress with a matching ribbon. He worked over-time every week to buy me a new dress to wear every Friday. He knew I loved dresses. I was very girly," Heather said smiling when she thought about her dad.

"I can't imagine you being girly," Kenneth said sarcastically.

"Anyway, all the girls had on pretty dresses hoping to win. Well, the fifth grade boys voted and I won by one vote. Crystal had a fit and she said that I stole the dress that I was wearing. She said I was poor and there was no way my family could afford my dress. I yelled at her and said she was a sore loser and that my daddy bought the dress for me because he loves me. I ran away crying," Heather said smiling.

"Well, what happened after that?" Kenneth asked leaning closer to her.

"Crystal ran after me and apologized. Then she invited me to her house for dinner and we became best friends. Her parents fell in love with me instantly."

"Yeah and so did Gabe," Kenneth said smiling.

"Why do you say that?" Heather said caught off guard by his observation of Gabe.

"Anybody can see that Gabe is in love with you. He has been since he was like twelve or thirteen years old. He's got it bad for you. Didn't you know?" Kenneth asked.

"I never noticed that he had a crush on me," Heather said asking for another drink. I guess I really did know; I just didn't want to see it when he was twelve, but I did notice when he was older.

"I guess you wouldn't notice a little twelve year old drooling over you when you were dating pretty boy Ricky," Kenneth said.

"I guess you know more about me than I realized," Heather said smiling.

"Crystal talks about you a lot. She really loves you like a sister. She's a true friend to you. Come to my car I have to show you something," Kenneth said getting up.

"Okay, I think it's time I get back home anyway," Heather said when she was getting up.

"Are you okay to drive?" Kenneth asked with concern. They were unaware that a pair of eyes had been watching them almost the entire time they were there. The person got up and called the Sterner house and told Crystal Sterner her best friend was having an affair with Kenneth and hung up the phone.

"Probably, I only had three or four drinks and they were pretty spread out," Heather said following him to the car.

"If you feel funny I'll take you home."

"What about the car?" Heather asked.

"You can send someone to get it on the morning if I take you home," Kenneth said.

"I guess so. What do you have to show me?" Heather asked.

"You have to get in the car first," Kenneth said.

"Alright," Heather said as Kenneth helped her in the car. He closed her door and ran to the other side and got in. He reached over her and opened his glove compartment. He took out a small box and opened it.

"This is for Crystal. I'm going to ask her to marry me when I think the time is right."

"That's so wonderful; Crystal is going to be so happy. She always wanted to get married and have kids. You guys are going to have a great life together. You can even tell your kids that you were a bad ass at one time," Heather said teasing him.

"So, you like the ring?" Kenneth asked.

"It's beautiful and Crystal will love it. I'd better head back home now. It was nice talking to you Kenneth," Heather said getting out of the car.

"Hey, can you drive home all right?" Kenneth asked getting out of the car following her to her car.

"I feel fine and thanks for the concern. If you're worried I'll call your cell phone when I get in. What's your number?" Heather asked. Kenneth gave her his number and she left. Heather drove home very slowly. She looked at the clock and it was almost one am. She hoped no one was worried about her. She made it home and she quietly made it back to her room. She turned on the light and Crystal was sitting in her bed.

Chapter Eleven

"Where have you been?" Crystal asked suspiciously.

"Out. Why do you want to know?" Heather said taking off her clothes.

"Who were you with?" Crystal nearly screamed.

"Why are you giving me the third degree? What's gotten into you?" Heather said really looking at her best friend.

"I know your secret you bitch. How could you, I thought we were best friends?" Crystal said with tears rolling down her cheeks.

"We are. I love you like a sister would. How did you find out?" Heather said sitting by Crystal hugging her.

"How could you do this to me? I never thought you would betray me in such a way. You have a fiancé, why do you need another man?" Crystal asked crying harder. She pushed Heather away from her.

"Crystal, did Gabe tell you this why I was out?" Heather asked.

"Gabe didn't tell me. It was someone else," Crystal said getting up from the bed.

"Who else could possibly know?" Heather asked with confusion.

"You mean Gabe knew and he didn't tell me," Crystal cried.

"Crystal, what are you talking about?" Heather asked

"What are you talking about?" Crystal asked.

"You go first since you were waiting on me," Heather said sitting at her vanity.

"Someone called me tonight and said that you were having an affair with Kenneth," Crystal said.

"And you believed them?" Heather screamed.

"Earlier you said that you had a secret and if you told me I would hate you forever. I thought about that after the call and I thought that's what your secret was," Crystal said feeling foolish suddenly.

"We've been best friends for almost sixteen years; you should know that I'd never betray you. I can't believe that you thought I would do that to you. You know better than that," Heather said with tears streaming down her face.

"I'm sorry, please forgive me," Crystal asked.

"You really do think I'm a slut. We'll I have some news for you. I'm the woman that slept with your brother and then broke his heart. I fucked his brains out the night of his college graduation. It was his congratulations present and then I left him high and dry," Heather said nastily.

"Why did you do that to him? You knew he was in love with you," Crystal said shocked by Heather's confession.

"Because I wanted him," Heather spat out with venom in her mouth.

"Do you have any idea what you put my brother

through you skinny bitch? He cried almost every day for several months straight. Can you imagine that, a grown man crying every day over a woman? He was like a zombie. It was terrible. We thought he was going to commit suicide. And all the time it was because of you. I can't believe that you did that," Crystal cried. She got out of the bed crossed the room and slapped Heather across her flawless face, "I want you out of this house right now. And for your knowledge I never thought of you as a slut up until now."

"Crystal, wait let me explain," Heather cried running after her best friend. Crystal spun around and waited for her to speak. Then she started to talk herself.

"Have you slept with him since you arrived here?"

"Yes, I slept with him twice," Heather said holding her head down

"What about your fiancé? Does he know your cheating on him?" Crystal screamed.

"No, I was going to tell him when he arrived into town."

"Some welcome, but lucky for you you're going back home tonight. You have an hour to get out of this house. You are no longer my best friend. I hate you. You are not the person I once knew and loved like a sister. Don't worry, I want tell my parents your dirty little secret or the reason for your sudden departure. I want them to have good memories of you," Crystal said and walked from the room. Heather lay on the bed and wept. The next morning she was gone. Crystal Sterner went into her ex-best friend's room, laid on the bed and wept.

Chapter Twelve

Crystal hard a light knock in the door. She got up from the bed and opened the door.

"What are you doing in here? Where is Heather?" Gabriel asked.

"She had to leave last night on an emergency," Crystal said.

"Well, she could've told everyone. When is she coming back?" Gabriel asked suspiciously.

"She didn't say when she's coming back. I'm sure she'll call when she can," Crystal said holding her head down.

"What's going on Crystal, where is Heather? I need to see, I mean speak to her," Gabriel said almost in a plea.

"You're still in love with her, aren't you?" Crystal asked.

"I don't know what you're talking about," Gabriel said looking away from his sister.

"Even after what she did to you. You still want to be with her," Crystal said to her brother.

"How do you know what happened between us?" Gabriel asked.

"Heather told me before she left. I'm sorry for what she put you through," Crystal said.

"Don't feel sorry for me. I loved every minute of what she did to me in that hotel room that night," Gabriel said as he sat on Heather's bed. He laid his head on her pillow hoping her scent was still there. Crystal looked at him with amazement. Her little brother was desperately in love with her best friend and she didn't know what to do about it. He would be upset if he knew the reason for Heather suddenly leaving, but she had to tell him the truth.

"Gabriel, Heather left because of me," she blurted out.

"What did you do to her?" he asked getting up from the bed with the pillow in his arms.

"I called her a slut for what she did to you and I told her to get out immediately. I ended our friendship and I told her that I never want to see her again," Crystal said with her head held down.

"How could you do that? She's not a slut and you know that. I want her to be my wife and the mother of my children," Gabriel said almost in a whisper.

"Gabriel, that's absurd and you know it. Heather has a fiancé and she's like six years older than you. What makes you think she wants to marry you?" Crystal asked.

"She doesn't want to marry me. I only wish she would. I called her a slut too and it broke her heart. Then, on top of that, you, her best friend in the entire world that she loves with all her heart called her a slut too. Wherever she is right now she's devastated. She'll never talk to anyone of us again," Gabriel yelled to his sister.

"Gabriel, calm down. Do you remember the hurt and the pain she caused you? You were heartbroken little brother and it was all her fault and then when she came here, she screwed your brains out again."

"That's none of your business what went on between her and I. And we didn't screw, we made love. I felt something when we were together and I think she felt it too. That's why she slept with me again, because she feels something for me," Gabriel said.

"You really love her, don't you?" Crystal asked.

"Yes, I do and I always will," Gabriel said laying back down on the bed.

"Gabriel, I accused her of having an affair with Kenneth," Crystal said.

"Why would say such a stupid thing? He's not even her type," Gabriel replied shaking his head.

"I wasn't thinking at the time. I felt stupid as soon as it came out of my mouth. I just lost the best friend I ever had," Crystal said with tears rolling down her face.

"You were just looking after your little brother. Thanks for the concern. It makes me feel special to know that you love me so much," Gabriel said getting up from the bed to hug his sister.

"Well, you are my little brother and I care about you. I can't believe that Heather did that to you. How could she be so cruel? I feel like I don't even know her anymore," Crystal said with tears still streaming down her face.

"But Crystal, she's still your best friend. You need to

talk to her and tell her how you feel and hear her side of everything," Gabriel said.

"I guess I'll have too, but I doubt if she'll talk to me. I really let her have it and plus I slapped her really hard. I think I left a bruise on her perfect face. I can't believe I hit her."

"I can't either, you're not a violent person, but I think she'll forgive you."

"She's was the one best friend I've ever had in the entire world and I just threw our friendship out of the door. She'll never talk to me again," Crystal replied.

"She'll talk to you because she adores you. You're the sister that she always wanted. I want to marry her Crystal and I need you to get her back here. I need her in my life. I can't function without her. I can't let her leave me again. I'll die if I can't see her again," Gabriel said almost in a plea.

"I had no idea your love for her was this serious. I'll get her back here for you, I promise," Crystal said walking out towards the door.

"Hey, don't tell mom and dad about me and Heather. I'd hate for them to feel animosity towards her."

"I won't tell them, I promise. Are you going to be all right?" Crystal asked her brother.

"I'll be fine. Just get her back to me," Gabriel said as he lay back on the bed to smell the scent of the woman he loved. Crystal took another look at her brother and she felt as if she would cry. She knew she had to get her best friend back even if it was just for Gabriel sake and not their friendship.

Chapter Thirteen

Heather looked at Stephen as he paced across the floor. He had the look of a murderer on his face. His fists were balled up at his sides and he looked as if he would explode in any minute.

"I can't believe you slept with her brother. How could you do that to me? I thought you cared about me?" Stephen shouted.

"I do care about you, but I'm not in love with you," Heather said.

"You could've told me that when I proposed to you. You know how much I love you. You mean the world to me. I want you to be my wife," Stephen said sitting beside Heather again.

"Stephen, I can't marry you. The marriage would never work. We would both be very miserable. I came here to tell you that it's over between us and to give you your ring back. I'm sorry for what I did to you and I wish you all the luck in the world," Heather said as she handed him the ring back.

"Please, Heather, don't leave me. I love you so much. I need you in my life," Stephen said as he grabbed her by the hand to stop her from leaving him.

"I have to go. My flight for Paris leaves in two hours," Heather said with tears in her eyes.

"You're going to Paris alone?" he asked suspiciously.

"Yes, I am. I need some time alone to clear my head. I'm not going to meet a man and have an affair. I just need to be alone. My best friend, I mean my ex-best friend hates me and now I have no one that cares for me," Heather said in heavy tears now.

"I care about you. You can always count on me. I don't care if you cheated on me. I still love you and I'll be your friend until the day I die," Stephen said taking her into his arms.

"Thank you, but I have to go. I have a plane to catch. I'll call you from Paris. And Stephen, I love you too," Heather said as she dried her face and left the apartment.

Chapter Fourteen

One month later.

"Heather, you can take a five minute break now," the photographer said to her.

"Okay, thank you Phil," Heather said as she dried the water from her face. She was on her second photo shoot of the day and she was tired. She was ready for another vacation, but she had nowhere to go or no one to visit. She felt very sad. Everyone she loved was gone. Two days earlier was the anniversary of her father's passing. She had stayed in her room and wept all day. She couldn't find it in her heart to fly home and visit his grave. It would've been too painful. She knew one day she would have to go back to visit or he would feel that he was forgotten by her. She no longer had her best friend or her best friend's family. She was still in love with Gabe, but she knew she could never have him. Every night in bed she dreamed about making love with him again and she could even feel his touches in her sleep. She longed to be with him and to have his children. She wanted him and she wanted her best friend back.

"That must be some daydream you're having. I'd give

any amount of money to know what it was about. I hope I was a part of it," someone said from behind her. Heather turned around and she was looking at the man she'd been dreaming of for the past month.

"What are you doing here?" She asked Gabriel.

"I came to see you. You look absolutely beautiful. How have you been?" He asked as he walked closer to her. He took the towel from her and wiped the last drops of water from her face.

"I'm fine. I've been very busy with photo shoots and traveling and talk shows," Heather managed to stammer out. All she could think about was how gorgeous he was. He looked like a Greek God.

"Yeah, I saw you on the daily show. You were so beautiful; I couldn't take my eyes off you. You look even prettier in person. What time is your shoot over today?" He asked.

"In one hour, why?" She asked.

"Because I need to talk to you in private about some very important things," he said in a very serious voice.

"Okay, meet me at the Bonifay Resort in an hour. My room is 817 on the eighteenth floor and I'll see you then. Here's my key so you can go ahead and go."

"I'll see you in an hour," Gabriel said as he walked away. He turned back around and walked over to her and kissed her passionately on the mouth and then he left. Heather stared at him for several minutes as he walked away. She thought to herself what he could possibly need to talk to her about. Was he really just there or was she daydreaming?

"Earth to Heather, earth to Heather. I'm ready to start shooting again whenever you are my love," Phil said glaring at her from the umbrella.

"I'm sorry Phil, I'm ready right now," Heather said as she made her way back to her spot to have her photos taken.

"Heather, you have to go to makeup first. Are you all right? Who was that man that just left?" Phil asked with concern.

"I'm fine; I just need to rest. It's been a very long day for me," Heather said as she made her way over to makeup.

She got home a little later than an hour. She knocked on her door because she didn't have her key and she almost fainted when she saw who opened the door.

"What are you doing here?" Heather demanded.

"I need to speak with you," her visitor replied.

"I guess you sent Gabe away because I'm a slut and he shouldn't be associated with me," Heather yelled.

"It was his idea for the switch. He thinks you and I should talk. We were best friends for several years and we should talk Heather," Crystal said laying her hand on her best friends shoulder

"Well, start talking, Crystal," Heather said as she snatched her shoulder away from Crystal's reach, "Actually, there's really nothing for you to say to me. I already know how you feel about me. You made it pretty clear last time you saw me. If you want me to stay away from your brother I will. I haven't spoken to him in a month. I didn't contact him. He came here looking for me."

"I'm sorry for the words that I said to you. I didn't mean them. I've been writing you letters for the past four weeks apologizing to you, but I had no idea where to send them too. I suppose I could've sent them to your usual address, but when I called you, you never answered. I figured you had moved. You do move alot and I thought you may have moved yet again. Last time we spoke I had no right to call you a slut and I blew up at you and I didn't give a chance to explain. I was upset with you for the way you treated my little brother. You broke his heart and if you had a little brother you would understand how I felt. I love Gabriel; he's my heart, Heather. Can't you understand that?" Crystal said sitting on the bed.

"Yes, I understand and I'm sorry too. I should not have lashed out at you about the way things went down between Gabe and me. I felt horrible for the way I told you what happened between Gabe and I. I didn't just fuck him. I made love to him and I fell in love. I'm in love with your brother and I have been for the past two years," Heather said with tears streaming down her face.

"Oh Heather, that's so wonderful. Gabriel came here hoping you'd tell him that you love him after he confessed his love for you again. This is so wonderful. If you guys get married you really will be my sister. That makes me so happy. I always wanted you to be my sister. My parents are going to be so happy," Crystal cried as she hugged Heather.

"How do you know that?" Heather asked.

"They always knew Gabriel was in love with you and they would always say that they wanted him to marry you," Crystal said with tears running down her face.

"Why haven't you ever told me that?" Heather asked.

"I didn't think you wanted to hear it."

"I may have been interested to know that. I do love your brother now. He's incredibly sexy and I want him for myself," Heather said.

"But Heather, whatever happened to Stephen?"

"I told him about my affair with Gabe and he took it pretty hard. He was very upset with me, but he still wanted to marry me. I felt so bad for the pain I caused him. I should've never took the ring from him or let our relationship go on for as long as it did. I knew I wasn't in love him from the beginning and I just strung him along. I loved him, but I was never in love with him. That was wrong of me," Heather said feeling very guilty.

"At least you didn't except his proposal and let the relationship go on any longer. Let me go downstairs and get Gabriel," Crystal said heading for the door.

"No, Crystal, let me go and get him. But first, what happened between you and Kenneth?" Heather asked.

"I told him about how I accused you of having an affair with him and he almost blew up. He said that I was crazy and I should've heard the way you talk about me at the bar. He said that you adored me and that you really love me. He asked me how could I be so stupid and cruel and he walked out on me," Crystal replied.

"I'm so sorry," Heather said.

"It's not your fault. I've always been jealous of you because you're so damn beautiful and perfect. Why would Kenneth want me when I have a beautiful supermodel as a best friend who's available?" Crystal asked with tears streaming in her eyes.

"Crystal, I would never betray you like that. You're my best friend and you have no reason to be jealous of me. In case you haven't noticed; you're beautiful too. Kenneth is in love with you and I know for a fact he's not interested in me," Heather snapped.

"How do you know?" Crystal asked.

"I just do. I could tell the way that he looks at you that he's head over heels in love with you. He adores you and I know things will work out for you," Heather said angrily, "And besides I'm not interested in him. I want Gabe."

"Heather, Kenneth and I made up anyway. I was just pulling your chain and trying to see if you really believed in our relationship," Crystal said with a smile wiping her fake tears away.

"You bitch; I should kick your ass. Give me a hug, so I can go downstairs," Heather said as she reached out to hug Crystal. They hugged and then Heather headed downstairs.

Chapter Fifteen

Heather made her way to the Hotel lobby and she spotted Gabe pacing back and forth. He looked very nervous and very sexy to Heather. For several moments she just watched him. He was such a beautiful specimen. As she watched him, she really saw for the first time that he was truly a man. He was so beautifully made. He had a wide chest and broad shoulders. He walked with pride and he was all male. He was absolutely beautiful and he was going to be all hers. She realized at that moment that she'd been in love with Gabriel Sterner since he was eighteen maybe even sixteen years old, when he would do all those stupid stunts to try to impress her. Her heart filled up with love. She walked up behind him and put her arms around him, "What are you so nervous for?"

"Hi, did you and my sister work everything out?" He asked as he pulled her in front of him.

"Yes, we're best friends as always. How did you find me?" Heather asked him as she looked him in the eyes with a big smile on her face.

"I have my sources."

"You have really good sources. No one can ever find me when I hide out."

I've missed you Heather," Gabriel said as he led her to a near-by bench.

"I've missed you too Gabe," she said in a very emotional voice.

"I need you in my life. The last time we spoke the words were not very nice. I apologize again for all the mean things I've ever said too you. Please forgive me," Gabe said as he kissed her forehead.

"I forgive you."

"Thank you," he said before kissing her on the forehead yet again.

"I hated the way we left each other. I'm sorry for the way I treated you."

"I know you are, we were both very emotional at the time."

"I fell in love with you the first time we slept together; actually, I think I was in love with you way before that."

"Are you serious?" Gabriel asked in disbelief.

"Yes, I just realized that earlier when I was watching you pace the room. I think I've always known; I was just in denial. I mean for goodness sake, you were my best friends annoying scrawny little brother. I couldn't possibly be in love with you right?" Heather asked teasingly.

"I guess not," Gabe said after pinching her on the side.

"I just thought that you should know that."

"Oh, well, thank you for telling me that. It makes me feel good inside."

"Your sister said you have something you need to ask me. What is it?" Heather asked.

"I ah...I was ah..." Gabe stammered because he couldn't get the words out. He was stunned at what she had just said about falling in love. He couldn't believe she'd been in love with him since he was sixteen. Heather the perfect gorgeous woman and supermodel was in love with him. Damn, how did I get so lucky? I can't wait to tell my friends.

"What is it?" Heather asked impatiently.

"Heather, you know I've been in love with you for nearly all of my life and I can't go another day without you," Gabe said as he got off the bench and kneeled down in front of her.

"Is that so?" Heather teased out even though she was near tears.

"Yes, I've wanted you damn near all my life. There has never been anyone else. Just you. Will you marry me?" Gabe asked her on one knee.

"Yes, Gabe, I'll marry you, but you have to grant me this one request first," Heather said.

"Anything, what is it?" Gabe asked getting up from the floor and taking her into his arms and spinning her around.

"You have to learn how to do the Cat Walk," Heather said laughing.

"I love you Heather."

"I love you too Gabriel Sterner. Now take me to my room and make sweet love to me."

"You don't have to tell me twice," Gabriel said as he led them to the elevator.

"This is going to be a great marriage," Heather said as she wrapped her arms around Gabriel's neck once they made it into the elevator.

"Oh, you have no idea," Gabriel said before they started kissing passionately once the elevator doors closed.

The End

CPSIA information can be obtained at www.ICGtesting.com
Printed in the USA
BVOW07s1154080714

358479BV00002B/379/P